What's for Breakfast?

What's for Breakfast?

DENYS CAZET

A NEAL PORTER BOOK
ROARING BROOK PRESS
NEW YORK

A Neal Porter Book
Published by Roaring Brook Press
Roaring Brook Press is a division of Holtzbrinck Publishing Holdings Limited Partnership
175 Fifth Avenue, New York, NY 10010
The artwork for this book was created using mixed media on watercolor paper.
mackids.com

Library of Congress Control Number: 2018931935
ISBN 978-1-250-17648-6

Our books may be purchased in bulk for promotional, educational, or business use. Please
contact your local bookseller or the Macmillan Corporate and Premium Sales Department
at (800) 221-7945 ext. 5442 or by e-mail at MacmillanSpecialMarkets@macmillan.com.

First edition, 2018
Book design by Jennifer Browne
Printed in China by RR Donnelley Asia Printing Solutions Ltd., Dongguan City, Guangdong Province

1   3   5   7   9   10   8   6   4   2

para
Carmelo Ramirez
y las muchachas

Yadira, Estefani,
Cassandra,
Carmelita y Lupita

Two owls sat on the window ledge of an old barn.
The little owl's name was Pip, and the big owl's
name was Rufus.

"Wake up!" said Rufus. "It's time to catch the fearsome mouse.
I'm in the mood for a wholesome bowl of mouse soup for breakfast."
"Too early," Pip grumbled.

"You need to practice your swooping," said Rufus.
"I'm not good at swooping," admitted Pip. "I'm good at sleeping."

"Listen!" whispered Rufus. "I hear a mouse! See? Over there at the foot of the big oak tree. Go . . . bring me something to mush . . . SWOOP!"

The little owl jumped off the window ledge. But . . .

when he tried to swoop . . .

. . . he crashed into the oak tree
and tumbled to the ground.

"OW!" he cried and pulled out
a lump he was sitting on. It was
the mouse. "Hey!" he shouted.
"I caught the fearsome mouse!"

"What's your name, fearsome mouse?"

"Theodore," squeaked the mouse.

"You don't look fearsome," said Pip. "You look small and sad."

"I am small . . . and I'm sad, because a big hungry owl fell out of the sky and sat on me in the middle of my breakfast!"

"I was swooping," said Pip.

"Pardon me for saying so," Theodore remarked, "but that was more falling than swooping."

"Yes, well . . . sleepy owls make sloppy swoopers!"

"At least you can fly," said Theodore.
"Once, I almost flew."
"No . . . really?"
"Sort of . . . I fell out of a tree."
"Falling is not flying," said Pip.

"Falling is not swooping, either," replied Theodore. "But if I could fly, I would fly above the tallest trees of the forest where the wind is the strongest. That's where I would practice my swooping."

The little owl looked up at the tops of the tallest pine trees swaying in the wind. He looked back at the mouse.

"I know what you're thinking," said Theodore. "What does someone as small as a mouse know?"

"We'll see!" said Pip. He grabbed
Theodore and flew off.

A warm gust of wind picked them up
and carried them higher and higher to the
farthest edges of the wildwood.
"Here goes!" Pip shouted.

They swooped past the empty windows of an abandoned farmhouse and across the meadow.

They swooped over the
pond, skimming the water.

And then they swooped
through the fading twilight,
skimming stars and the
rising moon.

When they landed, Pip set Theodore down.

"I swooped," panted the little owl.
"I flew," panted the little mouse.

Far away, they heard
a big owl calling.
"Uh-oh," gasped
Theodore. "I know
what that's about!"

The mouse opened a basket and looked inside. "Maybe he'd like something new to mush. It's good to try new things . . . like flying, or swooping from where the wind is the strongest."

"How about this?"

"What is that?"

"A banana," Theodore announced.

"Perfect for mushing!"

"We'll see," said Pip. He flew back to the barn.

The mouse flew back into his house.

"About time!" scolded Rufus. "I'm a very hungry owl!"

"Try this," said Pip.

"What is it? It doesn't have whiskers or a tail!"

"It's called a banana, perfect for mushing."

Rufus squeezed the banana. He tasted it. "Not bad. But to make a healthy breakfast soup, you need a dash of meadow mole."

The big owl stretched his wings and flew into the night.

"I swoop for soup!" he cried.

The little owl watched Rufus sail
past the cold light of the moon and
vanish into the shadows.

Below, at the foot of the oak tree,
he could see the warm light of the
mouse's lantern.

Pip wondered what else someone as small as
a mouse might know. And he wondered whether
Theodore had an extra banana.